This story is an adaptation of the puppet play *Bonne Fête Willy*
written by Marie-Louise Gay. The play, performed by the Théâtre
de l'Oeil of Montreal, has toured Canada since January 1989.
Marie-Louise Gay also designed the puppets, costumes, and sets of
Bonne Fête Willy.

Also by Marie-Louise Gay

Moonbeam on a Cat's Ear
Rainy Day Magic
Angel and the Polar Bear
Fat Charlie's Circus

Willy Nilly

MARIE-LOUISE GAY

For WT II

Stoddart

A Panda Picture Book

Published in 1995 by
Stoddart Publishing Co. Limited
34 Lesmill Road
Toronto, Canada
M3B 2T6

First published in hardcover in 1990

CANADIAN CATALOGUING IN PUBLICATION DATA

Gay, Marie-Louise
    Willy Nilly

Adaptation of the puppet play: Bonne fête Willy.
ISBN 0-7737-2429-X (bound) 0-7736-7433-0 (pbk.)

I. Title. II. Title: Bonne fête Willy.

PS8563.A95W53 1990   jC813'.54   C90-094400-5
PZ7.G39Wi   1990

Printed and bound in Hong Kong by Book Art, Toronto

Today is Willy Nilly's birthday.
He is seven years old, and he
just can't wait for his birthday party.
His mom told him to be patient
and to please go and play outside.

As Willy walked out the door,
he stumbled over a box,
a big box wrapped
in shimmery paper.
"Aha!" said Willy, "this must be
a present for me."
There was no card.
Willy hesitated, but it *was*
his birthday, so he ripped off
the paper and opened the box.
"A magician's game!" cried Willy.
The box was filled to the brim
with magic potions
and paper flowers,
scarves and mirrors
and sneezing powders.
There were balls and hoops
and a magician's hat,
playing cards and a plastic bat.
And at the very bottom,
The Great Book of Magic!

"Wow!" said Willy,
"I'm going to perform
every single trick in this book."
Willy started off with
the Magic Flower Trick.
It seemed really easy.
The idea was to pull a bouquet
of flowers
out of your sleeve.
Willy read
the magic formula:

"Alakazoo, alakazee,
scratch my nose, tickle my knee!"

Willy pulled and pulled.
He peered up his sleeve.
It was empty.
Just then... POOF! An enormous
bouquet of flowers
popped out of his ear!
"Oh dear!" said Willy,
"I guess I need to practice..."

"**W**illy!" yelled Tulip, his sister,
as she ran into the yard.
"What are you doing?"
"Rats!" thought Willy.
"Can't she ever leave me alone?"
"O-o-oh!" said Tulip,
"a magician's game!
Can I play with you?"
"No," said Willy, "go away. I'm busy."
"Please?" begged Tulip.
"No way!"
"Pretty please?" yelled Tulip.
"Okay, OKAY," said Willy,
"but you have to do exactly
what I say."
So Willy looked through his *Great
Book of Magic.*
"Let's see...how could I
make you disappear?"
"Oh no!" said Tulip.
"Scaredy-cat! Well, then,
this one looks great...
I'll turn you into a pink elephant!"
"Can you really do that?"
asked Tulip.
"Nothing to it!" Willy boasted.
"Here, drink this magic potion and...
*Alakazoo, alakazee,
scratch my nose, tickle my knee!*"

POOF!
Tulip disappeared in a cloud
of smoke. When it cleared,
Tulip had a beautiful
pink elephant head!
"Yu-u-uck!" said Tulip,
"that stuff tastes like old socks!"
Tulip examined her hands and feet.
"And it doesn't even work!
What a silly game! I don't want
to play anymore…"
And she stomped off into the house.
Willy stared after her.
"It worked!" he whispered.
"I don't believe it!
Boy, am I ever learning fast!"
That's when Marie looked
over the wall.

"Hey Willy!" called Marie,
"are you having a picnic?"
"Marie," said Willy,
"you won't believe this...
Tulip has an elephant head! I..."
"I don't believe you," said Marie.
"Can I eat with you?"
"It's true!" said Willy. "This is a
magician's game and I..."
"This looks delicious," said Marie.
"Is it strawberry juice?"
"Don't drink that!" cried Willy.
"It's magic potion!"
"You're nuts!" said Marie
as she took a sip.
"No-o-o!" yelled Willy,
"you silly fish-head!"
POOF!
Willy could not believe his eyes.
Marie had turned into a fish!
"What's the matter with you, Willy?"
said Marie. "Stop staring at me!
Boy! Are you ever weird today!"
"Uh... h-h-how are you feeling
Marie?" whispered Willy.
"Fine!" said Marie. "I'm going home
now. I feel like taking a bath."

"This is incredible!" thought Willy.
"I must be the most powerful
magician in the world!
I could be the king of
magicians! I could..."
"WILLY!" yelled Tulip.
"Something's wrong.
I can't blow my nose!"
"That's because you have
an elephant's head,"
Willy told her proudly.
"What!?" screamed Tulip.
"You are looking at a great magician,"
said Willy.
"Give me my head back,
right now!" said Tulip.
"But I want to call the reporters..."
"RIGHT NOW!" screamed Tulip.
"Okay, okay..." So Willy looked
in his *Great Book of Magic.*
   And looked. And looked.
   "Uh-oh," whispered Willy.
   Just then Marie came back.
"Anybody see any worms around
here? I'm so hungry."
"Her too?" said Tulip.
"What?" said Marie,
"what's the matter?"
"I can't find the antidote!"
said Willy miserably.

Willy's Aunt Mabel stuck her
head out the window.
"What's all the fuss about?"
she asked.
Willy told her the whole story.
He was pretty worried.
"Really! How interesting!"
said his aunt. "You have such
an imagination, Willy Nilly.
Let me see this magic potion.
Maybe I can help you."
Willy entered the house and
handed her the pink bottle.
"M-m-m, it smells good. I'll
just have a little taste."
"NO!" yelled Willy.
Too late.
POOF!
Aunt Mabel's ears grew very long
and very white.
Aunt Mabel's nose twitched.
Aunt Mabel had become a rabbit!
"Delicious!" Aunt Mabel
smacked her lips and fell asleep.
She even snored like a rabbit.

"Oh no! How will I ever get
out of this mess?"
moaned Willy. "I'll probably get
arrested and thrown in prison."
Willy went outside and stared
at the box.
"I should never have opened it,"
he thought.
Then Willy saw a little card
stuck on the side of the box.
It hadn't been there before.
It read:

Vladimir's
Magic and Mystery
33 Howlingcat Road

"Hey," thought Willy,
"maybe this Vladimir can help me."
So Willy ran down the street
towards Howlingcat Road.

Willy knocked on the door
at number 33.
It creaked open.
"Anybody home?" called Willy.
A fleet of bats flew
around his head.
"Hello-o-o..." they squeaked.
Willy screamed
and hid behind a box.
"Anybody home?" he whispered.
A deep voice boomed,
"Are you looking for me,
Willy Nilly?"
Willy looked up at the huge man
leaning over the counter.
"Are you Mr. Vladimir?"
"Maybe yes, maybe no...
How can I help you?"
asked Mr. Vladimir.
Willy told him the whole story.
How he had transformed his sister
into an elephant,
his best friend into a fish,
and his Aunt Mabel into a rabbit...
the whole terrible story.

"BRAVO!" said Vladimir,
"what a great magician you are!"
"But you don't understand,"
said Willy. "I'm in terrible trouble.
I can't find the antidote."
"The antidote? Whatever for?"
asked Mr. Vladimir.
"Think how powerful you are.
You will become rich and famous!
You will become
the king of magicians!
Isn't that what you wanted?"
"No, no!" said Willy. "Well,
maybe at first, but now I want
everything back to normal."
"Too bad!" sighed Mr. Vladimir,
and he reached under the counter
and brought up a bottle of
shiny green liquid. "Here is the
antidote…"
"Thank you!" cried Willy,
and he ran out of the store
clutching his precious bottle.
"Happy Birthday, Willy Nilly!"
Mr. Vladimir called out after him,
and chuckled softly to himself.

Willy ran into the yard
all out of breath.
"Tulip, Marie, Aunt Mabel!
Come here! I've got it!
I've got the antidote!"
"It's about time!" yelled Tulip.
Tulip and Marie helped Aunt
Mabel to hop outside and
they all took a swallow
of the shiny green potion.
POOF!
POOF!
POOF!
When the smoke cleared
   they all looked at each other
         and smiled.
      Then they saw Willy...
   and they roared
   with laughter!

Willy had Tulip's pink
elephant trunk.
Willy had Marie's fish tail
and bright green scales.
Willy had Aunt Mabel's
long white rabbit ears.
Willy looked pretty strange!
"O-O-OH NO!" cried Willy.
Just then Willy's mother called,
"Willy! It's time for your
birthday party."
"Quick!" said Willy,
"the antidote…"
The bottle was empty.
"Rats! This is horrible! I wish I had
never set eyes on this game!"
And Willy kicked the box
as hard as he could…
POOF!
The box disappeared
in a puff of smoke.
And Willy looked like
a seven-year-old boy again.
He smiled and ran into the house.
Everything was back to normal.

Well, almost...